P9-DCU-995
DATE DUE
4/18/01

BLACK
SCHOLASTIC PRESS NEW YORK

CAT

BY

CHRISTOPHER MYERS

to all children of the city, like me

Copyright © 1999 by Christopher Myers
All rights reserved. Published by Scholastic Press, a division
of Scholastic Inc., 555 Broadway, New York, New York, 10012.
Scholastic Press and colophon are trademarks of Scholastic Inc.

ISBN 0-590-03375-1
Library of Congress catalog card number: 98-28609
10 9 8 7 6 5 4 3 2 9/9 0/0 01 02 03
Printed in Mexico 49
First edition, April 1999

Book design by David Saylor. The art is a combination of photographs, collage, ink, and gouache. The text was set in 24 point Impact. Photographs developed by Alexis Mariel. Thanks, y'all.

black cat, black cat,
cousin to the concrete
creeping down our city streets
where do you live, where will we meet?

sauntering like rainwater down storm drains

between cadillac tires and the curb

sipping water from fire hydrants

dancing to the banging beats of passing jeeps

ducking under the red circling of sirens cutting

through the night

in the wake of sunday night families spilling

from blue neon churches

black cat, black cat, we want to know
where's your home, where do you go?

listening to brick music falling
from project windows

balanced like bottles somebody left on a wall

chasing subway mice
and platform rats

hearing the quiet language
of invisible trains

call
here.

ORDER TO SEE A
SEE A DOCTOR

black cat, black cat,
we want to know
where's your home,
where do you go?

leaving paw prints and chalk flowers

on concrete sidewalks

throwing shadows and tags

on graffiti-covered walls

leaping onto ledges

of bricked-in windows

eyes like the green

of empty glass bottles

mending city blocks cut by fences

playing chain-link games

black cat, black cat, we want to know
where's your home, where do you go?

crossing basketball courts and no-netted hoops

slam-dunking yourself

through a thin orange halo

watching children screaming in playground cages

tiptoeing across the click-clacking glow
of bodega lights

scraping paint from fire escapes

edging over rooftops

seeking sun-soaked spots

on hot tar beaches

black cat, black cat,

is there a place of your own?

we want to know,

where's your home?

black cat answers . . .

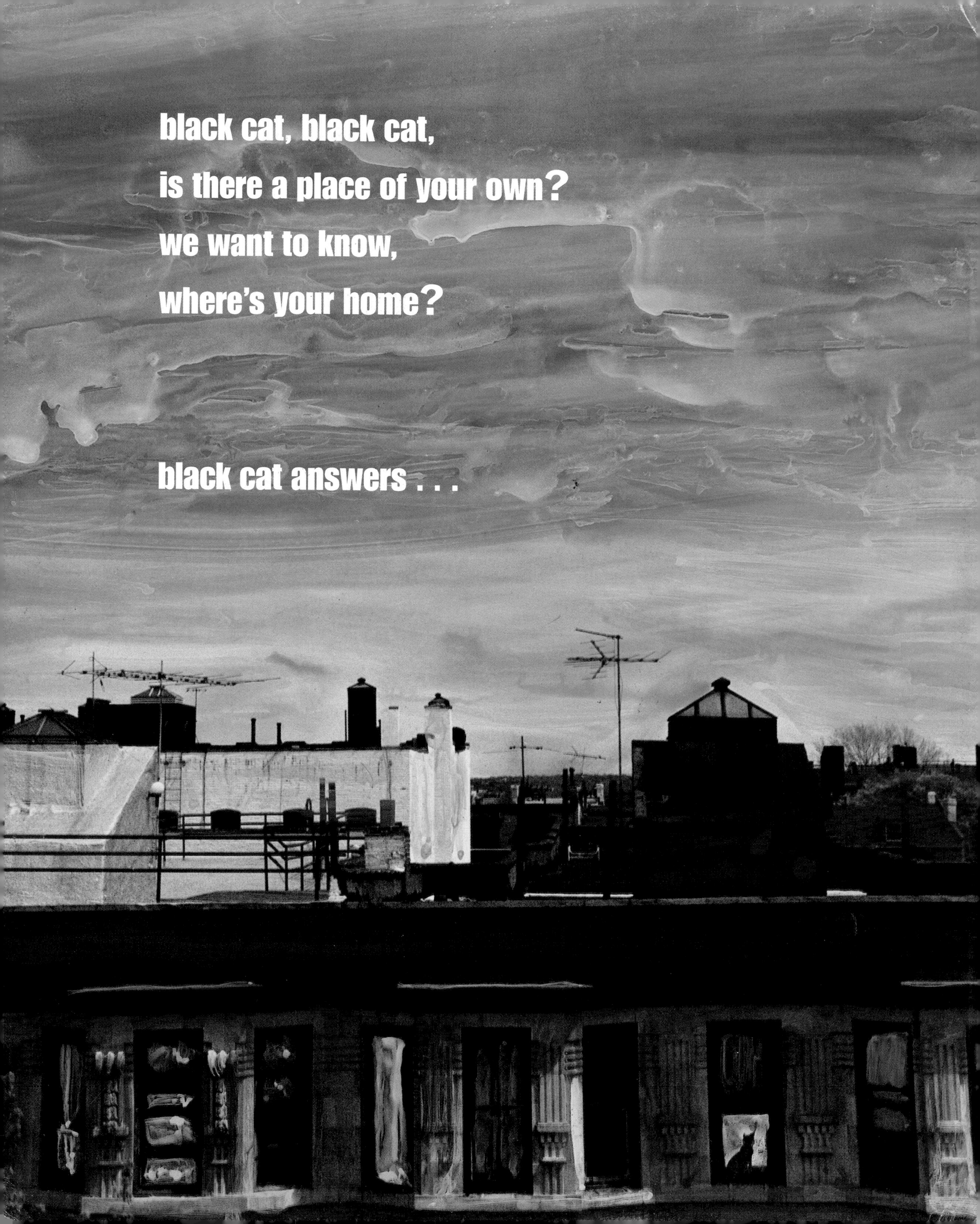

anywhere I roam.